The Backpack

Written by Roderick Hunt
Illustrated by Alex Brychta

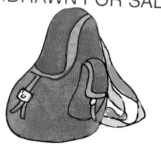

OXFORD
UNIVERSITY PRESS

Read these words

toy

backpack

ducks

rocket

pocket

boy

luck

pick

Chip was in a toy shop.

Wow! Lots of toys.

He put his backpack
by the ducks.

A boy put his backpack
by the ducks.

"Look at this rocket,"
said Chip.

8

"My cash is in my backpack," he said.

In the zip pocket.

Mum got a backpack.

But it was not Chip's backpack.

The boy had Chip's backpack.

Chip had the boy's backpack.

Chip was upset.

"Let's get it back," said Mum.

Mum and Chip ran ...

... to this shop ...

… to that shop.

The boy got on a bus.

"Stop that bus," said Mum.

The bus did stop.

Chip got his backpack back.

Talk about the story

Where did Chip put his backpack?

Where was Chip's cash?

Why did the boy pick up Chip's backpack?

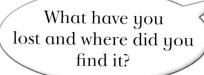

What have you lost and where did you find it?

A maze

Help Chip get to his backpack.